TALES of MAGIC and SPELLS

retold by
Corinne Denan

illustrated by
James Watling

Troll Associates

Tales of Magic and Spells: Beauty and the Beast, DeBeaumont; *Fisherman and His Wife*, Grimm; *Wild Swans*, Andersen.

Library of Congress# 79-66325
ISBN 0-89375-318-1/0-89375-317-3 (pb)

CONTENTS

Beauty and the Beast

Once upon a time there lived a rich, successful merchant who had three lovely daughters and three handsome sons. The youngest daughter was far more beautiful than her sisters. For this reason she was named Beauty. Her father adored her, for Beauty was goodhearted, kind, and gentle. But Beauty's two sisters were spoiled and bad-tempered. They were very jealous of Beauty and tried to make her life miserable.

One day a terrible misfortune befell the merchant. He received news that all of his ships with their cargoes had been lost at sea. His great fortune was gone. He had no choice but to move his family into a small cottage in the woods. And there they would live as peasants.

The sons helped their father to plow and sow the fields. They had to wear ragged clothes and live in a poor and simple way. The two selfish sisters did nothing but complain. "We are not used to this hard work," they said. "We are used to having servants do the work for us. It is not right that we dirty our hands and soil our clothes. We were not meant to labor as peasants."

Beauty, however, tried to help her father as

much as she could. So early every morning she cleaned the house, did the wash, and prepared breakfast for everyone.

Beauty tried to get her sisters to help with the chores, but they would do nothing. Because she was not as sad as they were, they believed that this miserable life was all she was fit for. But Beauty was too kind and good to let her selfish sisters disturb her.

Several years passed. Then one day the merchant received news that one of his richest cargo ships, believed to have been lost, had finally come safely into port. All the brothers and sisters rejoiced, for they knew that they could soon go back to their former way of life. They begged their father to bring them silk clothes and sparkling jewels from the town. But Beauty asked for nothing. This pleased her father, but he thought that such a beautiful young girl should have something pretty.

"Well, dear Father," she said, "if you insist, you may bring me a red rose. I have not seen one since we came here, and I love them very much."

The merchant set out for the town as quickly as possible. But, alas, upon his arrival he found that his former business partners, believing him to be dead, had already divided up the goods from the ship. And so, he was as poor as when he had started.

The merchant began the long journey home in bad weather. After he had traveled for many long hours, the wind began to blow harder, and the snow fell thick and heavy. The merchant was exhausted and feared he might freeze to death. He had lost his way in a dark forest.

Finally, he saw a small path and began to follow it. Before long, the path grew wider and the snow began to disappear. The air grew warm and pleasant, and at last, at the path's end, the merchant saw a splendid castle ablaze with lights.

He passed through magnificent courtyards filled with fragrant orange trees. Silence was all about him, and he did not see anyone at all. But he did see stables filled with grain and oats, and he led his weary horse inside and unsaddled it.

Then he climbed the beautiful marble stairs of the palace and wandered through splendidly furnished rooms and galleries. Still, he saw no one. He wondered who lived in such a beautiful place. Finally, he came upon a small room that had a fire burning. He sat down to wait for his unknown host, and he quickly fell into a deep sleep.

Upon awakening, the merchant saw that a little table spread with delicious food had been put

close to him. Since he had not eaten a thing for hours, he helped himself to some of the food.

Again the merchant fell asleep. He slept throughout the night, and awoke in the morning well rested. He ate the breakfast that he found next to him, and he put on fresh clothing. He wished that he might meet his host to thank him for his generosity. But he thought it best to begin the last part of his homeward journey.

The path leading to the stable was lined with the most exquisite rose hedges. They reminded the merchant of Beauty's request for a red rose. "At least one of my daughters will have her heart's desire," he thought to himself. And he bent over and picked a rose.

No sooner had he done so than he heard a strange noise behind him. He turned around, and there stood a horrible Beast. It was so terrible to look at, that the man shook with fright.

The Beast was furious. "You ungrateful, miserable man," he roared. "Isn't it enough that I fed you, clothed you, and gave you shelter? How dare you steal my roses?"

"It is for my youngest daughter, Beauty," the merchant answered. "I did not think you would mind."

"Of all my possessions, these roses are my

dearest," roared the Beast. "You shall pay for your evil deed. You shall be put to death!"

The merchant fell to his knees and begged forgiveness. "I meant no harm to you. I was just trying to grant my daughter her wish," cried the merchant. "Please do not kill me."

"I will forgive you on one condition," said the Beast. "Bring me one of your daughters. If you don't, you must come back alone, and then your life will be in my hands. Do not think you can hide from me. If you fail to return, I will come and find you."

The frightened merchant agreed to these terms. Although he did not want any one of his daughters to sacrifice her life for his, he was anxious to escape from the Beast. He promised to return in a month.

The merchant took Beauty's rose, and in no time at all, his horse carried him swiftly home. His children were delighted to see him after his long absence. But when they saw his face, they knew something was wrong. He handed the rose to Beauty and said, "Alas, little do you know what this rose has cost me."

Then he sat down wearily and told his children about everything that had happened to him. They tried to think of a way to outsmart the

Beast. But Beauty interrupted and said, "It was my desire for a rose that caused all this trouble. So I will go back with you, Father."

Her father and brothers grieved, for they truly loved Beauty and did not want her to go. But her two jealous sisters were only too glad that Beauty would finally be gone from their lives.

The month flew by. Beauty and her father readied themselves for the journey to the Beast's castle. They said tearful goodbyes and started on their way.

As they approached the palace, they could see that it was brightly lit from top to bottom. Beauty could not help but admire its splendor.

Together they went up the stairs and into the little room. Once again, the table had been laid with a delicious supper, which they ate, for the journey had made them very hungry.

As soon as they finished supper, they heard a loud noise. The Beast was approaching. How horrible he looked! Beauty trembled at the sight of him, but tried to conceal her fright.

Even though the Beast looked terrifying, he spoke in a very gentle manner. "Have you come here willingly?" he asked Beauty.

"Yes, I have," she replied bravely.

"I am pleased then," said the Beast. "You may

stay. As for you, old man," he said, turning to the merchant, "you must be prepared to leave tomorrow morning."

And with that the Beast bade them good night and went off to bed.

Beauty and her father spent the night comforting one another. In the morning, Beauty's father waved farewell and sadly left for home.

Beauty was now alone. She wandered through the castle until she came upon a room with her name on the door. Inside, she found splendid clothing and jewels. Everything she could desire was there. She began to realize that even though the Beast looked terrifying, he was kind and generous.

That evening, she wandered into the banquet hall and found the table prepared for her dinner. As she was eating, she heard the Beast approach.

"Good evening, Beauty. May I join you for dinner?" he asked.

"Of course," she replied. "You are master here."

"No, Beauty. You rule this castle. Your every desire is my command," said the Beast gently.

From then on, the Beast joined her for dinner every evening, and always brought her beautiful gifts. She began to look forward to his visits. And if he did not come to her, she went to him, for she no longer feared him.

One evening the Beast said to Beauty, "Do you really think me so ugly?"

Beauty had been taught always to tell the truth, so she replied, "Yes, Beast, I do think you are ugly."

Then he shocked her by asking, "Will you marry me and be my wife?"

"Oh, no!" replied Beauty. "I could not!"

The Beast shook his head sadly and went to bed. Every night he asked the same question, and every night Beauty answered "No."

The days and months passed, and Beauty found many amusements to occupy her time. She was happy. But one night she dreamed that her father was all alone and dying of grief for her. "I must return home to see him again," she thought. "I will ask the Beast for permission to-night."

The Beast now loved her so much that he did not want to see her unhappy. He agreed to let her go, but made her promise to return in two weeks. "If you do not return, it will be I who shall die of grief," said the Beast. "Can it be that you hate me that much?"

"Oh, no," replied Beauty. "I would be very sorry never to see you again. I shall be back in no time at all."

"Very well then, you shall be at your father's home tomorrow morning."

Then he placed a ring upon her finger, saying, "When you wish to return to my palace, turn this ring on your finger. Good night, Beauty. Sleep peacefully."

When Beauty awoke, she found herself at her father's cottage. Joy filled the merchant's heart at the sight of Beauty. Day by day, Beauty's father grew stronger because she was home again. But her sisters were jealous when they saw Beauty dressed like a princess. They begged her to stay home, saying how much they needed her. They hoped that she would break her promise to the Beast and lose the beautiful gifts he had given her. Beauty believed her sisters' lies, and so she stayed.

But as the days passed, Beauty missed the Beast and began to long for the palace.

Then one night she had a terrible dream. In her dream, she saw the Beast lying on a grassy path, dying of grief for her. A voice was saying, "This is what happens when people do not keep their promises!"

18

Beauty was so frightened by this dream that she immediately turned the ring and wished herself back in the palace. How good it felt to be there! She put on a lovely dress and waited anxiously for dinner time. She thought the day would never end. But that evening there was no sign of the Beast. She waited and waited.

Then, fearing her dream had come true, she rushed out into the garden to look for the Beast. She ran up and down, calling him in vain. Finally, she came upon the grassy path she had seen in her dream. And there lay the Beast, dying. Forgetting how ugly he was, she threw her arms around him. Then she drew some water from the fountain and sprinkled it on his face.

"Please do not die," she cried. "I never knew how much I loved you until now."

The Beast opened his eyes and said, "Oh, Beauty, I thought you had forgotten your promise to me. I cannot live without you. Will you marry me?"

"Oh, yes," replied Beauty. "I will be your wife."

As she spoke these words, the entire palace began to glow. At once, the Beast disappeared, and in his place stood a handsome young Prince.

"Where is my Beast?" cried Beauty.

"I was the Beast," replied the Prince. "Your words of love have broken the spell placed on me by a wicked witch. The spell could only be undone by someone who consented to marry me for what I was. You, dear Beauty, loved me for my heart, despite the way I looked."

Then Beauty and the Prince returned to the palace. The Prince sent for her father and brothers and sisters. Even her jealous sisters rejoiced in Beauty's happiness. The marriage took place soon afterward in great splendor, and Beauty and her handsome Prince lived happily ever after.

The Fisherman and his Wife

Once upon a time there was a fisherman and his wife who lived in a little hut close to the sea. He was a most unlucky fisherman, for every day he would fish and fish but never catch a thing. Then one day his luck changed. Something was tugging on the end of his line. As he pulled it into the boat, there on the hook was a great flounder.

To his amazement, the flounder began to talk to him.

"Please, fisherman, do not kill me! I am not a common flounder. I am an enchanted Prince under an evil spell! If you kill me I shall not be good to eat. Please put me back into the water, and let me live."

"Say no more," said the fisherman. "I could not bring myself to kill a fish that talks. I will let you go." Then he unhooked the flounder and tossed him back into the sea.

That night the fisherman returned to his little hut, empty-handed as usual. "Well, did you catch anything today?" asked his wife.

"I caught an unusual talking flounder, which I put back into the sea because he said he was an enchanted Prince," explained the fisherman.

His wife became angry. "An enchanted Prince, and you asked him for *nothing?*"

"I never thought of asking a favor," said the good fisherman.

"Alas," said his wife, "isn't it bad enough that we live in this tiny hut? You might at least have asked him for a pretty little cottage. Hurry back and call the flounder. You saved his life. Surely he will grant our wish."

The fisherman went back to the sea. He did not want to make his wife angrier than she was already. He found the sea no longer bright and shining, but dull and green. He stood in his boat and shouted:

"Flounder, flounder, in the sea,
I beg thee now to come to me.
My wife, it seems, must have her way.
She sends me for a favor this day."

Immediately, the flounder swam to the surface and said, "What favor does she ask?"

The fisherman replied, "She thinks I should have asked you for a wish when I caught you. She's tired of living in a little hut. She would like a pretty cottage."

"Return home then," said the flounder. "Her wish is granted."

The fisherman hurried home and found his wife standing in the doorway of a beautiful little cottage. Inside was a sitting room, a bedroom, and a kitchen filled with everything they could need. Outside was a little yard with chickens and a small vegetable garden.

"We can be content here for the rest of our lives," said the fisherman.

"We shall see about that," said his wife.

Everything went well for a week, and then one day the fisherman's wife said, "Husband, this cottage is too small. I would like to live in a huge stone castle. Go and ask the flounder for a castle."

The fisherman was perfectly content with the cottage. He felt his wife was being greedy. "I do not wish to go back," he said. "Perhaps the flounder will be angry with me."

"You saved his life," his wife yelled. "To grant this favor is the least he can do. Now go!"

Reluctantly, the fisherman returned to the sea. It was still calm, but it had become dark purple. He stood in his boat and called:

"Flounder, flounder, in the sea,
I beg thee now to come to me.
My wife, it seems, must have her way.
She sends me for a favor this day."

The flounder appeared again and said, "What does she want?"

"Alas," said the fisherman in a fearful voice, "my wife would like a big stone castle."

"Return home then," said the flounder. "Her wish is granted."

When the fisherman arrived home, he found a huge stone castle where the cottage had been. His wife greeted him at the door and said, "Come and see what's inside! It's splendid!"

The rooms were furnished with beautiful tables and chairs. There were rich tapestries and crystal chandeliers. Outside there was a magnificent courtyard with horses, stables, and grooms. Beautiful gardens with flowers and fruit trees were everywhere. Plenty of servants were there to attend to their every need.

"We will be content here for the rest of our lives," said the fisherman.

"We shall see about that," said his wife.

The next morning, the wife awoke at dawn and watched the sun come up over the beautiful countryside. She woke her husband by poking him, and said, "Wouldn't it be wonderful to rule over the whole countryside? We could live in a palace. Go to the flounder and tell him I want to be Queen."

"It is not right that we ask for more," said the fisherman. "Why do you want to be Queen?"

"Why shouldn't I be Queen?" she said angrily. "You saved the flounder's life. Now I insist you go."

So the fisherman went down to the sea with a heavy heart. Now the waters had become dark, rough, and foul smelling. He stood in his boat and called:

"Flounder, flounder, in the sea,

I beg thee now to come to me.

My wife, it seems, must have her way.

She sends me for a favor this day."

"Now what does she want?" asked the flounder.

"Alas," said the fisherman, "she wishes to be Queen."

"Return home then," said the flounder. "She is Queen already."

Upon returning home, the fisherman found that the castle had turned into a splendid palace. Soldiers guarded the doors, and inside everything was silver and gold. His wife sat on a high throne carved of ivory. On her head was a jeweled crown, and in her hand she carried a golden scepter. Her ladies-in-waiting stood on either side, each one shorter than the next.

"Well, Wife, are you now Queen?" asked the fisherman.

"Yes, I am Queen," she replied.

"This is a good thing. Now you will not wish for anything more," he said. "We will be content for the rest of our lives."

But to his dismay, his wife replied, "I am not content. I believe I will have too much time on my hands as Queen. I wish for something more. Now I want to be Empress. You must go back to the flounder."

"Alas," said the fisherman. "I will not ask this of the flounder. There is already an Empress ruling over these lands—why should there be two?"

"I am Queen now," cried the wife, "and you must take your orders from me. I mean to be Empress. Now go!"

The poor fisherman was frightened. "The flounder will be angry with me. This is not right." But rather than face his wife's anger, he went down to the sea. Now he found great black waves, and strong winds blowing everything to and fro. He stood in his boat and shouted:

"Flounder, flounder, in the sea,
I beg thee now to come to me.
My wife, it seems, must have her way,
She sends me for a favor this day."

"*Now* what does she want?" asked the flounder.

Frightened and trembling, the fisherman barely managed to say, "She wants to be Empress."

"Return home then," said the flounder. "Her wish is granted." And he quickly disappeared under a huge wave.

When the fisherman returned home, he came upon a palace made of polished marble, with the finest gold decorations. Soldiers and sentries stood guard. Inside the palace he found his wife sitting on a huge throne of solid gold. Upon her head was a tall golden crown covered with sparkling diamonds. In one hand she held a scepter, in the other a golden globe. Dukes, barons, and earls knelt before her.

The fisherman, still in a daze, went up to his wife and said, "Are you now Empress?"

"Yes," she replied. "I am Empress."

"Alas, my Wife," said the man. "Now you must be content, for you cannot go any higher." The fisherman was truly afraid of his wife's greed.

"We shall see about that," said his wife.

But all that night, the fisherman's wife tossed and turned. She could not sleep because she was thinking of what to ask for next. Finally, when the sun rose in the sky, she knew what she wanted.

"Wake up," she cried as she shook her husband impatiently. "I wish to cause the sun and moon to rise and set. I wish to command the stars in the sky. If I cannot do this, I shall never be happy again."

The fisherman was so startled by her words that he fell out of bed. "What did you say?" He could not believe what he had heard.

"I wish to be Master of the Universe. Go to the flounder and have him do this for me."

The frightened fisherman fell to his knees and begged his wife to reconsider. "The flounder will not be able to grant your wish this time. This is too much. Please be content with what you have now."

But his wife flew into a horrible rage. "You must obey me, for I am the Empress!" she screamed. "Remember that you once saved the flounder's life. He cannot refuse. Now be off with you!"

The fisherman ran down to the shore. He had never been so frightened. All around him a terrible storm raged. The sea and sky were black. There were mountainous waves. The wind blew through the trees, thunder crashed, and lightning flashed. He called out to the flounder, even

though he could hardly be heard above the roar:

"Flounder, flounder, in the sea,
I beg thee now to come to me.
My wife, it seems, must have her way.
She sends me for a favor this day."

"What does your wife want *now?*" asked the flounder.

The fisherman trembled all over. "She wants to be Master of the Universe," he cried.

"Return home then," replied the flounder. "She will get what she deserves."

When the fisherman returned home, gone was the splendid palace. Gone were the marble and gold decorations. Gone were the sparkling jewels. In their place stood the little hut with his wife at the doorway.

The flounder had returned everything to the way it had once been. And that is just the way it stayed.

The Wild Swans

This is a tale of a land far away and long ago. It was ruled by a King and Queen who had eleven sons and one daughter. As befitted royal children, the sons and daughter had everything they could desire. The eleven Princes wore golden stars on their garments and carried silver swords at their sides. Their beautiful young sister, the Princess Elise, had a crystal chair to sit on, and wrote with a diamond pencil on a golden slate.

But alas—their happy childhood days would soon draw to a close.

The children's mother died, and the King married a very wicked woman. The new Queen did not like the royal children. Through lies and tricks, she managed to turn the King against them. But the Queen wanted more—she wanted them out of her sight forever.

One day, because she was jealous of Elise's beauty, the wicked Queen sent the King's daughter to live with peasants far away, in the forest. Then, using her evil powers, she changed the Princes into eleven wild swans. She watched as they flew out the palace window, toward a land that was far, far away.

The years passed, and Elise became more beautiful with each passing day. But her heart was heavy as she thought of her brothers. Everything reminded her of the good times they had spent together. So she decided to leave the peasants' house and search for her brothers. She wandered through the lonely forest by day, and slept wherever she could find shelter at night. But her sleep was always troubled by dreams of her missing brothers.

One sunny morning, she came upon an old woman gathering berries. Elise asked her if she had seen eleven Princes riding through the forest.

"No," said the old woman. "But yesterday I saw eleven swans, swimming in the stream close by. They had golden crowns upon their heads."

Elise thanked the old woman and began to follow the winding stream. Soon she reached the spot where it flowed into the great open sea. There were no swans in sight. Elise felt very lonely. As she walked down to the shore, she saw eleven white feathers tangled in the seaweed. She gathered them and held them close to her heart.

That evening at sunset, Elise saw eleven white swans with golden crowns upon their heads flying toward the shore. She quickly hid behind some bushes and watched. As soon as the sun had disappeared from the sky, the swans turned into eleven handsome Princes. Elise had found her brothers. She ran to them, and at once they recognized her. They laughed and cried and embraced her.

Elise's eldest brother explained the curse of their evil stepmother. "We must fly as swans as long as the sun is above the horizon. When the sun goes down, we regain our human shapes. We must find a place to rest before each sunset, for if we should change back to humans while we are flying, we would plunge instantly to our deaths."

Then he told her about the land in which they lived. "It is across the ocean," he said. "But we are allowed to come here and visit our homeland only once each year—for eleven days. We fly over our father's palace, the place where we were born. And we look for you. Now at last we have found you. But, sadly, it is time for us to go back across the ocean."

"Take me with you," begged Elise.

"There is only one way," replied the brother. "We will have to carry you as we fly across the sea. But before dark, we must reach a certain rock that rises out of the sea. There we will rest."

And so they spent the night weaving a net of willow bark, bound together with rushes. Elise soon fell asleep on the net. When the sun rose, the brothers again became swans. They lifted the net carrying Elise, and flew high into the air.

When Elise awoke, she could not believe her eyes. She was high above the sea, far away from land. She ate the delicious berries her youngest brother had picked for her.

On and on they flew. The swans had to go slower than usual, for they had their sister to carry. When the sun was low in the sky, the rock was nowhere in sight. Elise was terribly frightened. If they could not reach the rock in time, they would fall into the sea, and she would be to blame. The sky became darker and darker. The wind began to blow hard, making their journey more difficult. The sun was sinking fast.

Suddenly the swans flew downward. Elise thought they were falling. But ahead she saw the tiny rock rising out of the water. It looked no bigger than a seal's head.

They landed safely and stood arm-in-arm together throughout the stormy night. At dawn, the air was fresh and still. The swans flew off with Elise once more.

Toward the end of the day, Elise saw the place

they sought. Great mountains and beautiful trees were everywhere. They landed by a large cave, and her brothers fixed a bed of soft, green moss for Elise. Thoughts of how she could free her brothers from their spell filled her mind.

In a dream that night, Elise once again met the old woman of the forest.

"I can tell you how to break the spell the evil Queen has cast over your brothers," said the old woman. "But you must have great courage, for you will suffer much pain. In the graveyard near this cave grow many sharp nettles like the one I hold in my hand. You must pick the nettles with your bare hands. Then crush the nettles with your bare feet until you have flax. From this flax you must weave eleven coats. Throw the coats over the eleven swans, and the spell will be broken. But from the moment you begin this work, until you finish, you must not speak a single word, even if it takes years. The first word you say will fall like a dagger through the hearts of your brothers!"

The eleven swans flew off at dawn. When Elise awoke, she found the nettles growing in the graveyard. She was overjoyed, for now she knew what she must do. She began to pick the sharp nettles.

When her brothers returned at sunset, they were saddened to find her silent. But when they saw her blistered hands, they knew she was doing this for their sake. Her youngest brother wept bitterly, and when his tears fell upon her hands, they caused the pain and blisters to disappear.

Elise worked on the coats day and night. She did not want to rest until her task was completed. One afternoon she was frightened by the loud sound of a hunting horn and the barking of dogs. They came closer and closer. Quickly, she sat upon her nettles and flax.

The dogs came bounding in, followed by huntsmen. The most handsome hunter was the King of the country. He was immediately taken with Elise's beauty.

"Why are you here, beautiful maiden?"

Elise dared not speak.

"Let me take you from this place," he said. "If you are as good as you are beautiful, I will dress you in silks and velvets. I will put a golden crown upon your head, and you shall live in my palace. I think only of your happiness." Then he lifted her upon his horse.

At the palace, Elise grieved for her unfinished work while the women dressed her in royal robes, placed pearls in her hair, and put soft gloves on her blistered hands. She was very beautiful, and the King begged her to be his bride. But she only looked sad.

Hoping to bring a smile to her lips, the King led her to a small room that had been made to look like the cave where he had found her. On the floor lay the bundle of flax she had spun from the nettles. "Here you may pretend you are in your other home. Perhaps this will make you happy," said the King.

Night after night, Elise worked in her tiny room, making one coat after another. But by the time she began the seventh coat, she had used up all her flax.

The following night, she crept quietly out of the palace and ran down to the graveyard to pick more nettles. It was dark and lonely, and she was frightened by the sound of the wind around the graves. But she gathered the stinging nettles and hurried back to the palace.

Unknown to Elise, the King's Counselor had seen her go to the graveyard. He believed she was a witch who had cast a spell over the King. The following morning he told the King what he had seen and what he believed.

"It is not so," cried the King. But there was a

tiny doubt in his heart. Every night he watched as Elise went down to her little room. He began to think his Counselor might be right.

Elise continued her task until she had just one more coat to finish. But again, she had used up all her flax. For the last time, she went to the graveyard to pick some nettles.

The King and the Counselor followed secretly behind her. When the King saw her moving about the graveyard, he believed she was indeed a witch making evil spells. With tears in his eyes he said, "Now the people must judge her." The following morning, the townspeople listened to the Counselor tell his story. They agreed that Elise must surely be a witch, and they condemned her to be burned at the stake.

Then Elise was led to a dark dungeon. She was given the stinging nettles for a pillow. The ten coats were thrown in a corner of the dungeon. She began work again, hoping to finish the last coat before dawn.

Just before sunset, she heard the sound of swans' wings outside her window. Her brothers had found her. She felt some comfort as she continued to work through the long night.

The next morning, the townspeople came to see the witch burn at the stake. Elise was taken from the dungeon in a horse-drawn cart. But even on the way to her death, she would not stop working on the last coat. Despite the jeers of the people, she worked hurriedly.

"Take her evil work away!" yelled the crowd. They gathered around her. Suddenly, eleven wild swans flew down and surrounded Elise.

As the executioner took her hand, Elise quickly threw the eleven coats over the swans. They changed instantly into eleven handsome Princes. But the youngest still had a swan's wing in place of an arm, for Elise had not been able to finish one sleeve of the eleventh coat.

"Now I may speak," cried Elise, "for the spell has been broken!"

Then the eldest brother told everyone the story of the wicked Queen's spell. There was great rejoicing everywhere. Bells began to ring. The King embraced Elise, and she consented to be his wife. Together, they led a happy procession back to the palace. And there they lived happily ever after.